THIS IS HAWKEYE

Written by *Clarissa Wong*

Illustrated by Andrea Di Vito *and* Rachelle Rosenberg

Based on the Marvel comic book series The Avengers

ABDO
Spotlight

MARVEL

Los Angeles
New York

ABDOPUBLISHING.COM

Reinforced library bound edition published in 2018 by Spotlight, a division of ABDO,
PO Box 398166, Minneapolis, Minnesota 55439. Spotlight produces high-quality
reinforced library bound editions for schools and libraries. Published by Marvel Press,
an imprint of Disney Book Group.

Printed in the United States of America, North Mankato, Minnesota.
042017
092017

marvelkids.com

THIS BOOK CONTAINS
RECYCLED MATERIALS

© 2014 MARVEL

LIBRARY OF CONGRESS CATALOGING-IN-PUBLICATION DATA

This title was previously cataloged with the following information:

Wong, Clarissa.
This is Hawkeye / written by Clarissa Wong ; illustrated by Andrea Di Vito and Rachelle
Rosenberg, based on the Marvel comic book series The Avengers.
  p. cm. -- (World of reading. Level 1)
Summary: Introduces Clint Barton, discusses how he became known as Hawkeye, and
shows how he contributes to the Avengers and S.H.I.E.L.D.
1. Hawkeye (Fictitious character : Lee)--Juvenile fiction. 2. Avengers (Fictitious
characters)--Juvenile fiction. 3. Superheroes--Juvenile fiction. 4. Avengers (Fictitious
characters) 5. Hawkeye (Fictitious character : Lee) 6. Superheroes.
PZ7.W8421 Th 2015
[E]--dc23
                     2014947425

978-1-5321-4052-5 (Reinforced Library Bound Edition)

Spotlight
A Division of ABDO
abdopublishing.com

This is Clint.

Clint is Hawkeye.

Hawkeye is a Super Hero.

Clint was not always a Super Hero.
He used to work in the circus.

He learned how to use
a bow and arrow there.
He was not very good at first.

Clint practiced every day.
He wanted to be the best.

Clint became a perfect shot.
People called him Hawkeye!

He could shoot very high.

He could shoot while upside down.

He could make any shot.

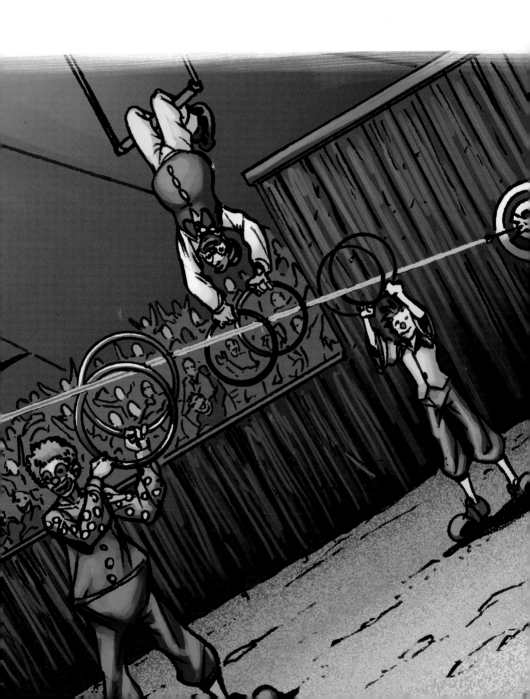

People came from far away
to see him!

He was the most popular act
in the circus.

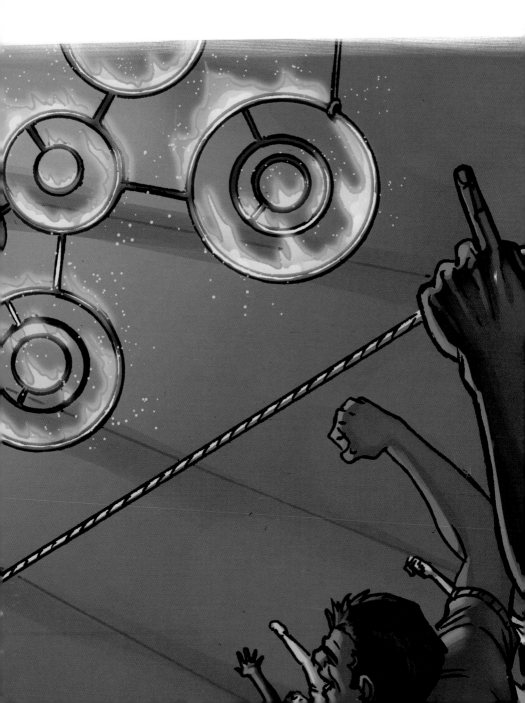

One day, Nick Fury came to see
the famous archer.
Fury was the leader of a group
called S.H.I.E.L.D.

Fury asked Hawkeye to be part
of S.H.I.E.L.D.!
Hawkeye is now a spy.
He is a secret agent.

He works with Black Widow.
They make a great team.

Together, they stop villains!

Watch out, villains!

Here come Hawkeye
and Black Widow!

They are best friends.
They joke around together.

They became Avengers, too.

Hawkeye can take out
crooks ...

. . . even if they are far away!

Iron Man helps Hawkeye
get a good angle.
They work as a team.

Hawkeye can get to places
no one else can.

He is always there to help!

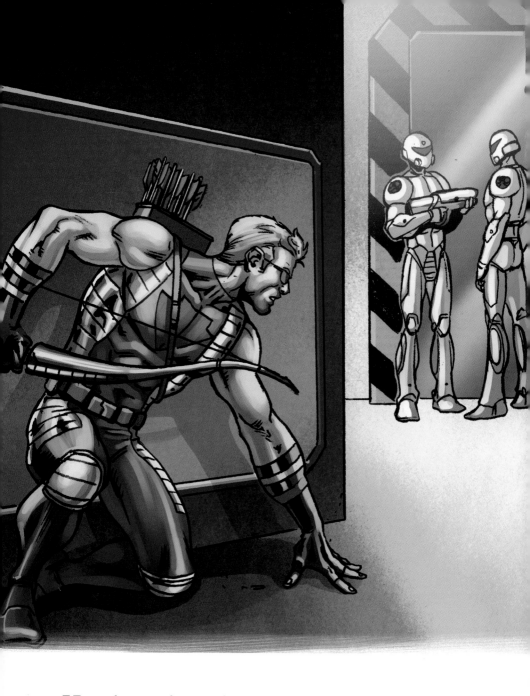

Hawkeye is quiet.
No one hears him coming.

He never misses his target.

That is because he is Hawkeye!